W9-COO-194

NATASHA WING'S
The Night Before
St. Patrick's Day

enter

shiny → treasure inside

Grosset & Dunlap
An Imprint of Penguin Random House

To elementary school teachers—my lucky charms!—NW

In memory of Pat Moyer.—AW

GROSSET & DUNLAP
Penguin Young Readers Group
An Imprint of Penguin Random House LLC

Text copyright © 2009 by Natasha Wing. Illustrations copyright © 2009 by Penguin Random House LLC. All rights reserved. Published by Grosset & Dunlap, an imprint of Penguin Random House LLC, 345 Hudson Street, New York, New York 10014. GROSSET & DUNLAP is a trademark of Penguin Random House LLC. Printed in the USA.

Library of Congress Control Number: 2008020699

ISBN 978-0-448-44852-7   10 9

NATASHA WING'S
The Night Before
St. Patrick's Day

By Natasha Wing
Illustrated by Amy Wummer

Grosset & Dunlap
An Imprint of Penguin Random House

'Twas the night before St. Patrick's—

the day to wear green.

Not a creature was stirring,

except Tim and Maureen.

They decked out the den
from ceiling to floor
with streamers and rainbows
and shamrocks galore.

Later they carefully made traps
with gold charms and rings.

"I bet we catch a leprechaun.
They love shiny things."
For if they caught one—
so the legend told—
they'd find where he buried
his big pot of gold.

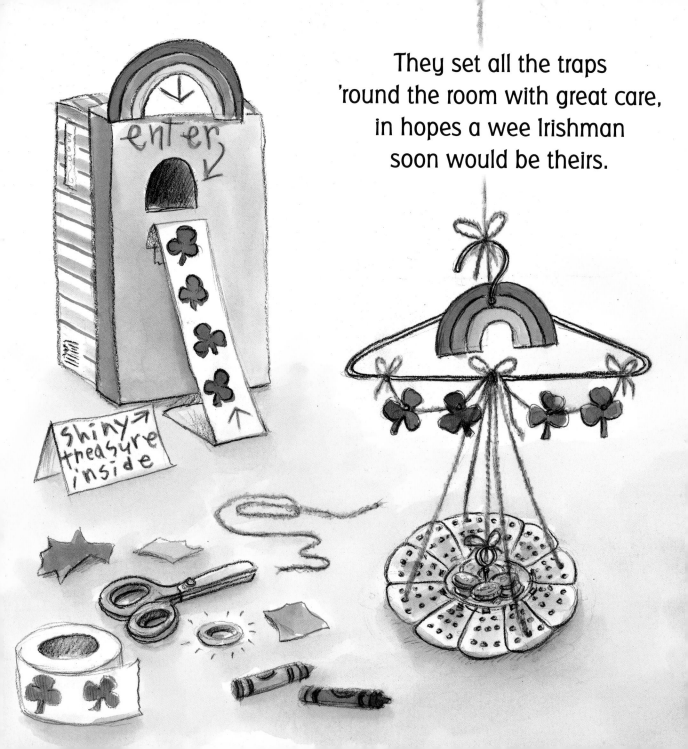

They set all the traps
'round the room with great care,
in hopes a wee Irishman
soon would be theirs.

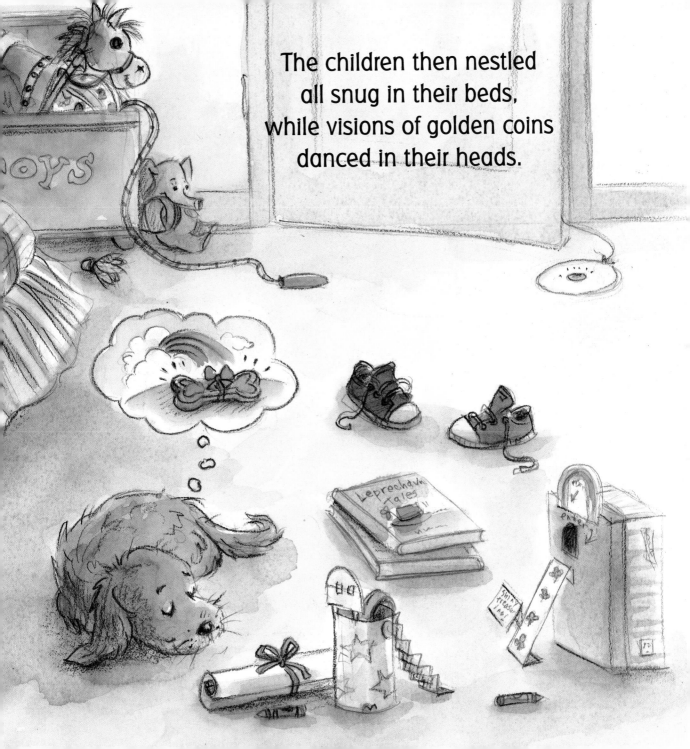

The children then nestled
all snug in their beds,
while visions of golden coins
danced in their heads.

"Happy St. Paddy's!" said Dad
early the next morning.
Then he started to play
bagpipes without warning.

He huffed and he puffed
an old Irish song.

Mom dished out
green eggs

and sang loudly
along.

When, from their bedroom,
there arose such a clatter,
the kids ran down the hallway
to see what was the matter.

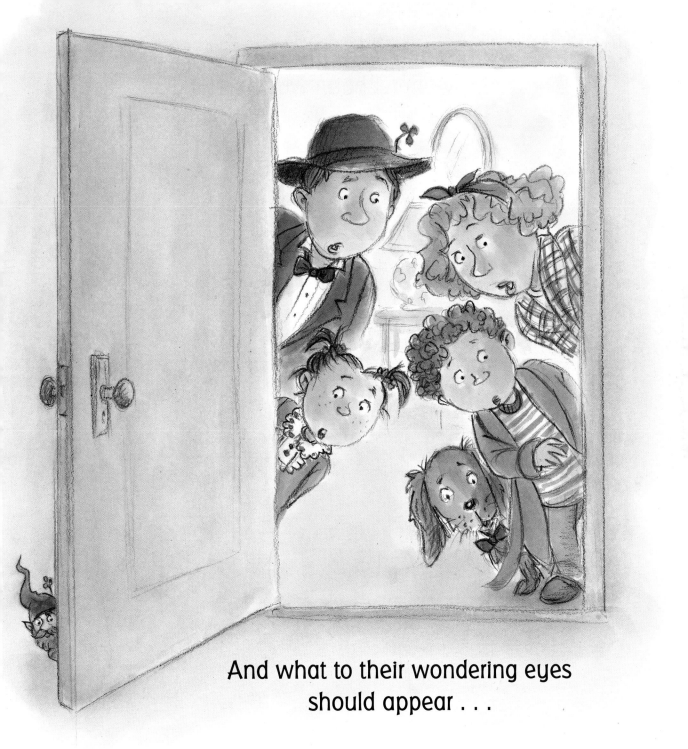

And what to their wondering eyes
should appear . . .

. . . but a terrible mess.
A leprechaun was here!

"Be quiet," whispered Maureen.
"He's hiding somewhere.
When we find him, remember,
we must hold his stare."
For if you look away,
if you so much as blink,
leprechauns vanish,
quick as a wink.

The kids trailed muddy footprints
back and forth 'cross the floor . . .

which led them under Tim's bed
and past the closet door.

And then, inside a trap,
they heard someone giggling.
A real live leprechaun!
They both saw him wriggling.

His eyes—how they twinkled! His body so tiny!

His hand clasped a trinket so golden and shiny!
He was dressed in all green, from his head to his toes,
and he looked like a cobbler wearing fairy-sized clothes.

The children approached him,
staring straight in his eyes.
"Tell us where the gold is.
Don't be tricky—no lies!"

"I buried it under a rock,
smooth and hard.
It's marked with an *X*
right in your backyard."

But when the kids went outside
with their shovel and pick,

they instantly saw
it had been a big trick!

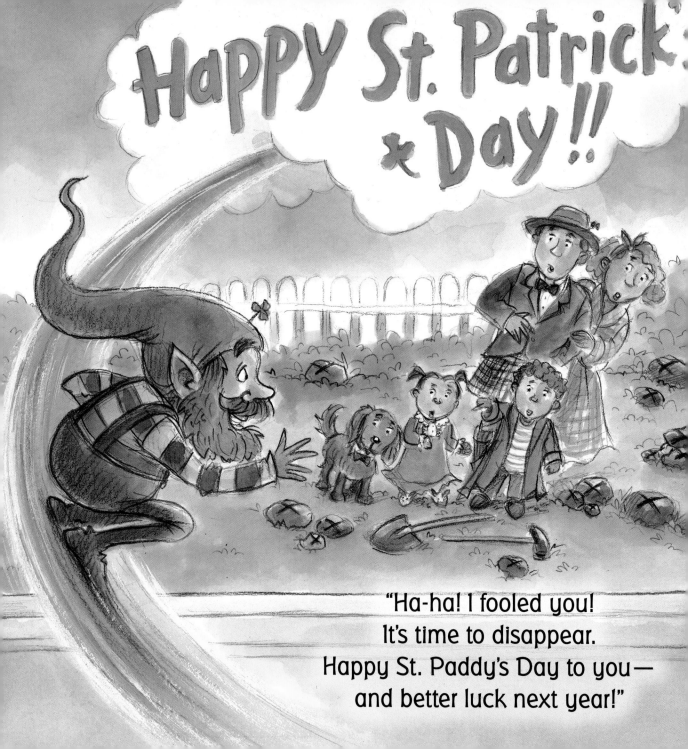